GRANDFATHER DUCK

Written & Illustrated by
KEVIN O'MALLEY

muddy boots™

we jump in puddles

Guilford, Connecticut

Published by Muddy Boots
An imprint of The Rowman & Littlefield Publishing Group, Inc.
4501 Forbes Blvd., Ste. 200
Lanham, MD 20706

MuddyBootsBooks.com

Distributed by NATIONAL BOOK NETWORK

British Library Cataloguing-in-Publication Information available

Library of Congress Control Number: 2017918198
ISBN 978-1-63076-335-0 (hardcover)
ISBN 978-1-63076-336-7 (e-book)

♾ The paper used in this publication meets the minimum requirements of
American National Standard for Information Sciences—Permanence of Paper for
Printed Library Materials, ANSI/NISO Z39.48-1992.

Printed in Selangor Darul Ehsan, Malaysia
May 2018

AT THE QUACK OF DAWN THE DUCKLINGS WOKE UP.

And just like every morning things got a little crazy.

Gilbert ran around yelling, "Outside, outside, outside!"

Dilbert said, "Look at me, I'm flying!"

And Rosco asked, "What's for lunch, what's for lunch?"

Grandfather Duck and Mother Duck looked at each other.

"What do you get when you cross fireworks with a duck?" asked Grandfather.

"I don't know, Dad," said Mother Duck.

"A Fire Quacker," said Grandfather.

"Pop?" asked Mother Duck. "Pop, could you take the ducklings out? I have many things to do around here today."

"Of course I will, my dear."

Grandfather stood up straight and saluted his daughter.

"I'll take them to the park!"

"Gentlemen, it's time.
Line up outside and count off!"

Gilbert raced to the gate. "Outside, outside, outside!"

Dilbert raced to the gate. "Look at me, look at me, look at me. I'm flying!"

Rosco raced to the gate. "What's for lunch, what's for lunch, what's for lunch?"

They all quacked up when they got to the gate.

"Are you guys okay or should I take you to the Ducktor?" asked Grandfather.

"Gentlemen, I need you to do as I do. Everybody walk this way."

Grandfather Duck did a funny little walk.

All the ducklings did the same.

They passed by the old cow.

"Where are you going?" asked the cow.

"We are going to get something to eat," said Grandfather.

"How will you pay for it?" asked the cow.

"I'll put it on my bill," said Grandfather.

The ducklings tried to stay in line but they had a hard time.

Gilbert started running ahead yelling, "Outside, outside, outside!"

Dilbert put out his little wing and spun around in circles. "Look at me, look at me, look at me. I'm flying!"

And Rosco raced ahead. "What's for lunch, what's for lunch, what's for lunch?"

"Gentlemen," yelled Grandfather, "it's time to line up and count off again.

"Everybody walk this way."

Grandfather Duck did a funny little walk again.

All the ducklings did the same.

When they reached the pond Rosco yelled,
"What's for lunch, what's for lunch, what's for lunch?"

He started to eat everything he could see.

He was about to eat some mushrooms.

Grandfather raced over to him.

"Easy now, boy. Everything is edible, but some things are only edible once."

Grandfather showed Rosco the best and the safest things to eat at the pond.

They snacked on flowers and roots.

"Outside, outside, outside!" yelled Gilbert.

Grandfather could hear him but he couldn't see him.

He raced into the bushes.

Hiding behind a tree was a cat who was about to pounce on Gilbert.

Grandfather raised his wings and quacked very loud.

The cat ran away.

Grandfather led Gilbert out of the bushes.

"Some mistakes are too much fun and you might make them more than once. Some mistakes you can ONLY make just once."

Gilbert and Grandfather talked about the trees and the bushes and the sky and the pond.

"Look at me, look at me, look at me. I'm going to fly!"

Dilbert stood on the top of a very large rock.

"Quack!" yelled Grandfather and he raced over to him.

"Dilbert get down from there."

Dilbert didn't listen and he jumped.

THUMP.

He hit the ground.

"Are you okay?" asked Grandfather. "Failure is not falling down. It is not getting up again. Come with me, my boy."

They walked over to some rocks by the pond.

"Spread out your wings. Get your legs ready to jump."

Dilbert didn't fly the first time, but he landed in the water with a laugh.

"Again, again, again!" he yelled.

The ducks played by the pond all day.

Grandfather ran and chased and quacked. He didn't have a chance to rest his webbed feet.

As the sun was setting he called out,
"Okay, gentlemen, line up and count off.
It's time to head home."

"Boy, you boys were gone a long time," said Mother Duck.

"Did you have a good time?"

Mother Duck asked,

"Did you go to the pond?

Did you go for a swim?

Did you get something to eat?

Were the ducklings good?

Did you have fun?"

But Grandfather couldn't hear her.

Grandfather and the ducklings had fallen asleep.